THE PENGUIN POETS

# HOUSEBOAT DAYS

John Ashbery was born in Rochester in 1927, grew up on a farm in western New York State, and was educated at Deerfield Academy, Harvard, and Columbia, where he specialized in English literature. In 1955 he went to France, where he wrote art criticism for the Paris *Herald Tribune*. He returned to New York in 1965, was Executive Editor of *Art News* until 1972, and now teaches English at Brooklyn College. His books of poetry include *Turandot and Other Poems, Some Trees, The Tennis Court Oath, Rivers and Mountains, The Double Dream of Spring, Three Poems*, and most recently, *Self-Portrait in a Convex Mirror*. He has written plays and essays and is co-author, with James Schuyler, of a novel, *A Nest of Ninnies*. He was awarded the Pulitzer Prize, the National Book Award, and the National Book Critics Circle Award for *Self-Portrait in a Convex Mirror*.

# Houseboat Days

POEMS BY

## John Ashbery

PENGUIN BOOKS

Penguin Books Ltd, Harmondsworth,
Middlesex, England
Penguin Books, 625 Madison Avenue,
New York, New York 10022, U.S.A.
Penguin Books Australia Ltd, Ringwood,
Victoria, Australia
Penguin Books Canada Ltd, 2801 John Street,
Markham, Ontario, Canada  L3R 1B4
Penguin Books (N.Z.) Ltd, 182–190 Wairau Road,
Auckland 10, New Zealand

First published in the United States of America
in simultaneous hardbound and paperbound editions by
The Viking Press and Penguin Books 1977

ISBN 0-14-042.202-1

Printed in the United States of America by
Murray Printing Company, Westford, Massachusetts
Set in Linotype Janson

Grateful acknowledgment is made to the following publications, in
which these poems first appeared: *American Poetry Review*: "Variant,"
"The Couple in the Next Room," "Lost and Found and Lost Again,"
and "Saying It to Keep It from Happening." *Antaeus*: "Crazy
Weather" and "Bird's-Eye View of the Tool and Die Co." *Chicago
Review*: "All Kinds of Caresses" and "The Thief of Poetry." *Denver
Quarterly*: "Unctuous Platitudes" and "On the Towpath." *Georgia
Review*: "Loving Mad Tom" and "Whether It Exists." *New York
Review of Books*: "Valentine," "Houseboat Days," "Street Musicians,"
"The Gazing Grain," "Wet Casements," and "Friends." *The New
Yorker*: "Melodic Trains," "Collective Dawns," "The Lament upon
the Waters," and "The Wrong Kind of Insurance." *Poetry*: "The Ice-
Cream Wars," "Blue Sonata," "Syringa," and "Fantasia on 'The
Nut-Brown Maid.' " *Roof*: "Two Deaths." *The Scotsman*: "The
Explanation." *Spectator*: "And *Ut Pictura Poesis* Is Her Name." *Sun*:
"And Others, Vaguer Presences." *Times Literary Supplement*: "Busi-
ness Personals" and "Daffy Duck in Hollywood." *Vanderbilt Poetry
Review*: "What Is Poetry." *Yale French Studies*: "Drame Bourgeois."
Z: "The Other Tradition" and "Wooden Buildings."

"The Serious Doll" was first published by the Kermani Press. "Pyrog-
raphy" was commissioned by the U.S. Department of the Interior for
its Bicentennial exhibition, "America 1976," and first appeared in the
exhibition catalog published by the Hereward Lester Cooke Foundation.

# Table of Contents

*Houseboat Days*

# Street Musicians

One died, and the soul was wrenched out
Of the other in life, who, walking the streets
Wrapped in an identity like a coat, sees on and on
The same corners, volumetrics, shadows
Under trees. Farther than anyone was ever
Called, through increasingly suburban airs
And ways, with autumn falling over everything:
The plush leaves the chattels in barrels
Of an obscure family being evicted
Into the way it was, and is. The other beached
Glimpses of what the other was up to:
Revelations at last. So they grew to hate and forget each
   other.

So I cradle this average violin that knows
Only forgotten showtunes, but argues
The possibility of free declamation anchored
To a dull refrain, the year turning over on itself
In November, with the spaces among the days
More literal, the meat more visible on the bone.
Our question of a place of origin hangs
Like smoke: how we picnicked in pine forests,
In coves with the water always seeping up, and left
Our trash, sperm and excrement everywhere, smeared
On the landscape, to make of us what we could.

# The Other Tradition

They all came, some wore sentiments
Emblazoned on T-shirts, proclaiming the lateness
Of the hour, and indeed the sun slanted its rays
Through branches of Norfolk Island pine as though
Politely clearing its throat, and all ideas settled
In a fuzz of dust under trees when it's drizzling:
The endless games of Scrabble, the boosters,
The celebrated omelette au Cantal, and through it
The roar of time plunging unchecked through the sluices
Of the days, dragging every sexual moment of it
Past the lenses: the end of something.
Only then did you glance up from your book,
Unable to comprehend what had been taking place, or
Say what you had been reading. More chairs
Were brought, and lamps were lit, but it tells
Nothing of how all this proceeded to materialize
Before you and the people waiting outside and in the next
Street, repeating its name over and over, until silence
Moved halfway up the darkened trunks,
And the meeting was called to order.

                                        I still remember
How they found you, after a dream, in your thimble hat,
Studious as a butterfly in a parking lot.
The road home was nicer then. Dispersing, each of the
Troubadours had something to say about how charity
Had run its race and won, leaving you the ex-president

Of the event, and how, though many of those present
Had wished something to come of it, if only a distant
Wisp of smoke, yet none was so deceived as to hanker
After that cool non-being of just a few minutes before,
Now that the idea of a forest had clamped itself
Over the minutiae of the scene. You found this
Charming, but turned your face fully toward night,
Speaking into it like a megaphone, not hearing
Or caring, although these still live and are generous
And all ways contained, allowed to come and go
Indefinitely in and out of the stockade
They have so much trouble remembering, when your
    forgetting
Rescues them at last, as a star absorbs the night.

# *Variant*

Sometimes a word will start it, like
Hands and feet, sun and gloves. The way
Is fraught with danger, you say, and I
Notice the word "fraught" as you are telling
Me about huge secret valleys some distance from
The mired fighting—"but always, lightly wooded
As they are, more deeply involved with the outcome
That will someday paste a black, bleeding label
In the sky, but until then
The echo, flowing freely in corridors, alleys,
And tame, surprised places far from anywhere,
Will be automatically locked out—*vox
Clamans*—do you see? End of tomorrow.
Don't try to start the car or look deeper
Into the eternal wimpling of the sky: luster
On luster, transparency floated onto the topmost layer
Until the whole thing overflows like a silver
Wedding cake or Christmas tree, in a cascade of tears."

# Collective Dawns

You can have whatever you want.
Own it, I mean. In the sense
Of twisting it to you, through long, spiralling afternoons.
It has a sense beyond that meaning that was dropped there
And left to rot. The glacier seems

Impervious but is all shot through
With amethyst and the loud, distraught notes of the cuckoo.
They say the town is coming apart.
And people go around with a fragment of a smile
Missing from their faces. Life is getting cheaper

In some senses. Over the tops of old hills
The sunset jabs down, angled in a way it couldn't have
Been before. The bird-sellers walk back into it.
"We needn't fire their kilns; tonight is the epic
Night of the world. Grettir is coming back to us.
His severed hand has grabbed the short sword
And jumped back onto his wrist. The whole man is waking
    up.
The island is becoming a sun. Wait by this
Mistletoe bush and you will get the feeling of really
Being out of the world and with it. The sun
Is now an inlet of freshness whose very nature
Causes it to dry up." The old poems
In the book have changed value once again. Their black letter

Fools only themselves into ignoring their stiff, formal
    qualities, and they move
Insatiably out of reach of bathos and the bad line
Into a weird ether of forgotten dismemberments. Was it
This rosebud? Who said that?

The time of all forgotten
Things is at hand.
Therefore I write you
This bread and butter letter, you my friend
Who saved me from the mill pond of chill doubt
As to my own viability, and from the proud village
Of bourgeois comfort and despair, the mirrored spectacles
    of grief.
Let who can take courage from the dawn's
Coming up with the same idiot solution under another guise
So that all meanings should be scrambled this way
No matter how important they were to the men
Coming in the future, since this is the way it has to happen
For all things under the shrinking light to change
And the pattern to follow them, unheeded, bargained for
As it too is absorbed. But the guesswork
Has been taken out of millions of nights. The gasworks
Know it and fall to the ground, though no doom
Says it through the long cool hours of rest
While it sleeps as it can, as in fact it must, for the man to
    find himself.

# *Wooden Buildings*

The tests are good. You need a million of them.
You'd die laughing as I write to you
Through leaves and articulations, yes, laughing
Myself silly too. The funniest little thing . . .

That's how it all began. Looking back on it,
I wonder now if it could have been on some day
Findable in an old calendar? But no,
It wasn't out of history, but inside it.
That's the thing. On whatever day we came
To a small house built just above the water,
You had to stoop over to see inside the attic window.
Someone had judged the height to be just right
The way the light came in, and they are
Giving that party, to turn on that dishwasher
And we may be led, then, upward through more
Powerful forms of poetry, past columns
With peeling posters on them, to the country of
 indifference.
Meanwhile if the swell diapasons, blooms
Unhappily and too soon, the little people are nonetheless
 real.

# *Pyrography*

Out here on Cottage Grove it matters. The galloping
Wind balks at its shadow. The carriages
Are drawn forward under a sky of fumed oak.
This is America calling:
The mirroring of state to state,
Of voice to voice on the wires,
The force of colloquial greetings like golden
Pollen sinking on the afternoon breeze.
In service stairs the sweet corruption thrives;
The page of dusk turns like a creaking revolving stage in
    Warren, Ohio.

If this is the way it is let's leave,
They agree, and soon the slow boxcar journey begins,
Gradually accelerating until the gyrating fans of suburbs
Enfolding the darkness of cities are remembered
Only as a recurring tic. And midway
We meet the disappointed, returning ones, without its
Being able to stop us in the headlong night
Toward the nothing of the coast. At Bolinas
The houses doze and seem to wonder why through the
Pacific haze, and the dreams alternately glow and grow dull.
Why be hanging on here? Like kites, circling,
Slipping on a ramp of air, but always circling?

But the variable cloudiness is pouring it on,
Flooding back to you like the meaning of a joke,
The land wasn't immediately appealing; we built it
Partly over with fake ruins, in the image of ourselves:
An arch that terminates in mid-keystone, a crumbling stone
    pier
For laundresses, an open-air theater, never completed
And only partially designed. How are we to inhabit
This space from which the fourth wall is invariably missing,
As in a stage-set or dollhouse, except by staying as we are,
In lost profile, facing the stars, with dozens of as yet
Unrealized projects, and a strict sense
Of time running out, of evening presenting
The tactfully folded-over bill? And we fit
Rather too easily into it, become transparent,
Almost ghosts. One day
The birds and animals in the pasture have absorbed
The color, the density of the surroundings,
The leaves are alive, and too heavy with life.

A long period of adjustment followed.
In the cities at the turn of the century they knew about it
But were careful not to let on as the iceman and the milkman
Disappeared down the block and the postman shouted
His daily rounds. The children under the trees knew it
But all the fathers returning home
On streetcars after a satisfying day at the office undid it:
The climate was still floral and all the wallpaper
In a million homes all over the land conspired to hide it.
One day we thought of painted furniture, of how
It just slightly changes everything in the room
And in the yard outside, and how, if we were going
To be able to write the history of our time, starting with
    today,
It would be necessary to model all these unimportant details

So as to be able to include them; otherwise the narrative
Would have that flat, sandpapered look the sky gets
Out in the middle west toward the end of summer,
The look of wanting to back out before the argument
Has been resolved, and at the same time to save appearances
So that tomorrow will be pure. Therefore, since we have to
   do our business
In spite of things, why not make it in spite of everything?
That way, maybe the feeble lakes and swamps
Of the back country will get plugged into the circuit
And not just the major events but the whole incredible
Mass of everything happening simultaneously and pairing
   off,
Channeling itself into history, will unroll
As carefully and as casually as a conversation in the next
   room,
And the purity of today will invest us like a breeze,
Only be hard, spare, ironical: something one can
Tip one's hat to and still get some use out of.

The parade is turning into our street.
My stars, the burnished uniforms and prismatic
Features of this instant belong here. The land
Is pulling away from the magic, glittering coastal towns
To an aforementioned rendezvous with August and
   December.
The hunch is it will always be this way,
The look, the way things first scared you
In the night light, and later turned out to be,
Yet still capable, all the same, of a narrow fidelity
To what you and they wanted to become:
No sighs like Russian music, only a vast unravelling
Out toward the junctions and to the darkness beyond
To these bare fields, built at today's expense.

# The Gazing Grain

The tires slowly came to a rubbery stop.
Alliterative festoons in the sky noted
That this branchy birthplace of presidents was also
The big frigidaire-cum-cowbarn where mendicant

And margrave alike waited out the results
Of the natural elections. So any openness of song
Was the plainer way. O take me to the banks
Of your Mississippi over there, etc. Like a plant

Rooted in parched earth I am
A stranger myself in the dramatic lighting,
The result of war. That which is given to see
At any moment is the residue, shadowed

In gold or emerging into the clear bluish haze
Of uncertainty. We come back to ourselves
Through the rubbish of cloud and tree-spattered pavement.
These days stand like vapor under the trees.

# Unctuous Platitudes

There is no reason for the surcharge to bother you.
Living in a city one is nonplussed by some

Of the inhabitants. The weather has grown gray with age.
Poltergeists go about their business, sometimes

Demanding a sweeping revision. The breath of the air
Is invisible. People stay

Next to the edges of fields, hoping that out of nothing
Something will come, and it does, but what? Embers

Of the rain tamp down the shitty darkness that issues
From nowhere. A man in her room, you say.

I like the really wonderful way you express things
So that it might be said, that of all the ways in which to

Emphasize a posture or a particular mental climate
Like this gray-violet one with a thin white irregular line

Descending the two vertical sides, these are those which
Can also unsay an infinite number of pauses

In the ceramic day. Every invitation
To every stranger is met at the station.

# The Couple in the Next Room

She liked the blue drapes. They made a star
At the angle. A boy in leather moved in.
Later they found names from the turn of the century
Coming home one evening. The whole of being
Unknown absorbed into the stalk. A free
Bride on the rails warning to notice other
Hers and the great graves that outwore them
Like faces on a building, the lightning rod
Of a name calibrated all their musing differences.

Another day. Deliberations are recessed
In an iron-blue chamber of that afternoon
On which we wore things and looked well at
A slab of business rising behind the stars.

# The Explanation

The luxury of now is that the cancelled gala has been
Put back in. The orchestra is starting to tune up.
The tone-row of a dripping faucet is batted back and forth
Among the kitchen, the confusion outside, the pale bluster
Of the sky, the correct but insidious grass.
The conductor, a glass of water, permits all kinds
Of wacky analogies to glance off him, and, circling outward,
To bring in the night. Nothing is too "unimportant"
Or too important, for that matter. The newspaper and the
    garbage
Wrapped in it, the over, the under.
                                    You get thrown to one side
Into a kind of broom closet as the argument continues
    carolling
Ideas from the novel of which this is the unsuccessful
Stage adaptation. Too much, perhaps, gets lost.
What about arriving after sunset on the beach of a
Dank but extremely beautiful island to hear the speeches
Of the invisible natives, whose punishment is speech?

At the top of his teddy-bear throne, the ruler,
Still lit by the sun, gazes blankly across at something
Opposite. His eyes are empty rectangles, shaped
Like slightly curved sticks of chewing gum. He witnesses.
But we are the witnesses.

In the increasingly convincing darkness
The words become palpable, like a fruit
That is too beautiful to eat. We want these
Down here on our level. But the tedium persists
In the form of remarks exchanged by birds
Before the curtain. What am I doing up here?
Pretending to resist but secretly giving in so as to reappear
In a completely new outfit and group of colors once today's
Bandage has been removed, is all.

# Loving Mad Tom

You thought it was wrong. And afterwards
When everyone had gone out, their lying persisted in your
    ears,
Across the water. You didn't see the miserable dawns piled
    up,
One after the other, stretching away. Their word only
Waited for you like the truth, and sometimes
Out of a pure, unintentional song, the meaning
Stammered nonetheless, and your zeal could see
To the opposite shore, where it was all coming true.

Then to lay it down like a load
And take up the dream stitching again, as though
It were still old, as on a bright, unseasonably cold
Afternoon, is a dream past living. Best to leave it there
And quickly tiptoe out. The music ended anyway. The
    occasions
In your arms went along with it and seemed
To supply the necessary sense. But like
A farmhouse in the city, on some busy, deserted
    metropolitan avenue,
It was all too much in the way it fell silent,
Forewarned, as though an invisible face looked out
From hooded windows, as the rain suddenly starts to fall
And the lightning goes crazy, and the thunder faints dead
    away.

That was a way of getting here,
He thought. A spear of fire, a horse of air,
And the rest is done for you, to go with the rest,
To match up with everything accomplished until now.
And always one stream is pointing north
To reeds and leaves, and the stunned land
Flowers in dejection. This station in the woods,
How was it built? This place
Of communicating back along the way, all the way back?
And in an orgy of minutes the waiting
Seeks to continue, to begin again,
Amid bugs, the barking of dogs, all the
Maddening irregularities of trees, and night falls anyway.

# Business Personals

The disquieting muses again: what are "leftovers"?
Perhaps they have names for it all, who come bearing
Worn signs of privilege whose authority
Speaks out of the accumulation of age and faded colors
To the center of today. Floating heart, why
Wander on senselessly? The tall guardians
Of yesterday are steep as cliff shadows;
Whatever path you take abounds in their sense.
All presently lead downward, to the harbor view.

Therefore do your knees need to be made strong, by
    running.
We have places for the training and a special on equipment:
Knee-pads, balancing poles and the rest. It works
In the sense of aging: you come out always a little ahead
And not so far as to lose a sense of the crowd
Of disciples. That were tyranny,
Outrage, hubris. Meanwhile this tent is silence
Itself. Its walls are opaque, so as not to see
The road; a pleasant, half-heard melody climbs to its ceiling—
Not peace, but rest the doctor ordered. Tomorrow . . .
And songs climb out of the flames of the near campfires,
Pale, pastel things exquisite in their frailness
With a note or two to indicate it isn't lost,
On them at least. The songs decorate our notion of the world
And mark its limits, like a frieze of soap-bubbles.

What caused us to start caring?
In the beginning was only sedge, a field of water
Wrinkled by the wind. Slowly
The trees increased the novelty of always being alone,
The rest began to be sketched in, and then . . . silence,
Or blankness, for a number of years. Could one return
To the idea of nature summed up in these pastoral images?
Yet the present has done its work of building
A rampart against the past, not a rampart,
A barbed-wire fence. So now we know
What occupations to stick to (scrimshaw, spinning tall
    tales)
By the way the songs deepen the color of the shadow
Impregnating your hobby as you bend over it,
Squinting. I could make a list
Of each one of my possessions and the direction it
Pointed in, how much each thing cost, how much for wood,
    string, colored ink, etc.

The song makes no mention of directions.
At most it twists the longitude lines overhead
Like twigs to form a crude shelter. (The ship
Hasn't arrived, it was only a dream. It's somewhere near
Cape Horn, despite all the efforts of Boreas to puff out
Those drooping sails.) The idea of great distance
Is permitted, even implicit in the slow dripping
Of a lute. How to get out?
This giant will never let us out unless we blind him.

And that's how, one day, I got home.
Don't be shocked that the old walls
Hang in rags now, that the rainbow has hardened
Into a permanent late afternoon that elicits too-long
Shadows and indiscretions from the bottom
Of the soul. Such simple things,

And we make of them something so complex it defeats us,
Almost. Why can't everything be simple again,
Like the first words of the first song as they occurred
To one who, rapt, wrote them down and later sang them:
"Only danger deflects
The arrow from the center of the persimmon disc,
Its final resting place. And should you be addressing
   yourself
To danger? When it takes the form of bleachers
Sparsely occupied by an audience which has
Already witnessed the events of which you write,
Tellingly, in your log? Properly acknowledged
It will dissipate like the pale pink and blue handkerchiefs
That vanished centuries ago into the blue dome
That surrounds us, but which are, some maintain, still here."

# *Crazy Weather*

It's this crazy weather we've been having:
Falling forward one minute, lying down the next
Among the loose grasses and soft, white, nameless flowers.
People have been making a garment out of it,
Stitching the white of lilacs together with lightning
At some anonymous crossroads. The sky calls
To the deaf earth. The proverbial disarray
Of morning corrects itself as you stand up.
You are wearing a text. The lines
Droop to your shoelaces and I shall never want or need
Any other literature than this poetry of mud
And ambitious reminiscences of times when it came easily
Through the then woods and ploughed fields and had
A simple unconscious dignity we can never hope to
Approximate now except in narrow ravines nobody
Will inspect where some late sample of the rare,
Uninteresting specimen might still be putting out shoots,
    for all we know.

# On the Towpath

At the sign "Fred Muffin's Antiques" they turned off the
    road into a narrow lane lined with shabby houses.

If the thirst would subside just for awhile
It would be a little bit, enough.
This has happened.
The insipid chiming of the seconds
Has given way to an arc of silence
So old it had never ceased to exist
On the roofs of buildings, in the sky.

The ground is tentative.
The pygmies and jacaranda that were here yesterday
Are back today, only less so.
It is a barrier of fact
Shielding the sky from the earth.

On the earth a many-colored tower of longing rises.
There are many ads (to help pay for all this).
Something interesting is happening on every landing.
Ladies of the Second Empire gotten up as characters from
    Perrault:
Red Riding Hood, Cinderella, the Sleeping Beauty,
Are silhouetted against the stained-glass windows.
A white figure runs to the edge of some rampart
In a hurry only to observe the distance,

And having done so, drops back into the mass
Of clock-faces, spires, stalactite machicolations.
It was the walking sideways, visible from far away,
That told what it was to be known
And kept, as a secret is known and kept.

The sun fades like the spreading
Of a peacock's tail, as though twilight
Might be read as a warning to those desperate
For easy solutions. This scalp of night
Doesn't continue or break off the vacuous chatter
That went on, off and on, all day:
That there could be rain, and
That it could be like lines, ruled lines scored
Across the garden of violet cabbages,
That these and other things could stay on
Longer, though not forever of course;
That other commensals might replace them
And leave in their turn. No,

We aren't meaning that any more.
The question has been asked
As though an immense natural bridge had been
Strung across the landscape to any point you wanted.
The ellipse is as aimless as that,
Stretching invisibly into the future so as to reappear
In our present. Its flexing is its account,
Return to the point of no return.

# Melodic Trains

A little girl with scarlet enameled fingernails
Asks me what time it is—evidently that's a toy wristwatch
She's wearing, for fun. And it is fun to wear other
Odd things, like this briar pipe and tweed coat

Like date-colored sierras with the lines of seams
Sketched in and plunging now and then into unfathomable
Valleys that can't be deduced by the shape of the person
Sitting inside it—me, and just as our way is flat across
Dales and gulches, as though our train were a pencil

Guided by a ruler held against a photomural of the Alps
We both come to see distance as something unofficial
And impersonal yet not without its curious justification
Like the time of a stopped watch—right twice a day.

Only the wait in stations is vague and
Dimensionless, like oneself. How do they decide how much
Time to spend in each? One begins to suspect there's no
Rule or that it's applied haphazardly.

Sadness of the faces of children on the platform,
Concern of the grownups for connections, for the chances
Of getting a taxi, since these have no timetable.
You get one if you can find one though in principle

You can always find one, but the segment of chance
In the circle of certainty is what gives these leaning
Tower of Pisa figures their aspect of dogged
Impatience, banking forward into the wind.

In short any stop before the final one creates
Clouds of anxiety, of sad, regretful impatience
With ourselves, our lives, the way we have been dealing
With other people up until now. Why couldn't
We have been more considerate? These figures leaving

The platform or waiting to board the train are my brothers
In a way that really wants to tell me why there is so little
Panic and disorder in the world, and so much unhappiness.
If I were to get down now to stretch, take a few steps

In the wearying and world-weary clouds of steam like great
White apples, might I just through proximity and aping
Of postures and attitudes communicate this concern of mine
To them? That their jagged attitudes correspond to mine,

That their beefing strikes answering silver bells within
My own chest, and that I know, as they do, how the last
Stop is the most anxious one of all, though it means
Getting home at last, to the pleasures and dissatisfactions
    of home?

It's as though a visible chorus called up the different
Stages of the journey, singing about them and being them:
Not the people in the station, not the child opposite me
With currant fingernails, but the windows, seen through,

Reflecting imperfectly, ruthlessly splitting open the bluish
Vague landscape like a zipper. Each voice has its own
Descending scale to put one in one's place at every stage;
One need never not know where one is

Unless one give up listening, sleeping, approaching a small
Western town that is nothing but a windmill. Then
The great fury of the end can drop as the solo
Voices tell about it, wreathing it somehow with an aura

Of good fortune and colossal welcomes from the mayor and
Citizens' committees tossing their hats into the air.
To hear them singing you'd think it had already happened
And we had focused back on the furniture of the air.

# Bird's-Eye View
## of the Tool and Die Co.

For a long time I used to get up early.
20-30 vision, hemorrhoids intact, he checks into the
Enclosure of time familiarizing dreams
For better or worse. The edges rub off,
The slant gets lost. Whatever the villagers
Are celebrating with less conviction is
The less you. Index of own organ-music playing,
Machinations over the architecture (too
Light to make much of a dent) against meditated
Gang-wars, ice cream, loss, palm terrain.

Under and around the quick background
Surface is improvisation. The force of
Living hopelessly backward into a past of striped
Conversations. As long as none of them ends this side
Of the mirrored desert in terrorist chorales.
The finest car is as the simplest home off the coast
Of all small cliffs too short to be haze. You turn
To speak to someone beside the dock and the lighthouse
Shines like garnets. It has become a stricture.

# Wet Casements

The conception is interesting: to see, as though reflected
In streaming windowpanes, the look of others through
Their own eyes. A digest of their correct impressions of
Their self-analytical attitudes overlaid by your
Ghostly transparent face. You in falbalas
Of some distant but not too distant era, the cosmetics,
The shoes perfectly pointed, drifting (how long you
Have been drifting; how long I have too for that matter)
Like a bottle-imp toward a surface which can never be approached.
Never pierced through into the timeless energy of a present
Which would have its own opinions on these matters,
Are an epistemological snapshot of the processes
That first mentioned your name at some crowded cocktail
Party long ago, and someone (not the person addressed)
Overheard it and carried that name around in his wallet
For years as the wallet crumbled and bills slid in
And out of it. I want that information very much today,

Can't have it, and this makes me angry.
I shall use my anger to build a bridge like that
Of Avignon, on which people may dance for the feeling
Of dancing on a bridge. I shall at last see my complete face
Reflected not in the water but in the worn stone floor of my bridg

I shall keep to myself.
I shall not repeat others' comments about me.

# Saying It to Keep It from Happening

Some departure from the norm
Will occur as time grows more open about it.
The consensus gradually changed; nobody
Lies about it any more. Rust dark pouring
Over the body, changing it without decay—
People with too many things on their minds, but we live
In the interstices, between a vacant stare and the ceiling,
Our lives remind us. Finally this is consciousness
And the other livers of it get off at the same stop.
How careless. Yet in the end each of us
Is seen to have traveled the same distance—it's time
That counts, and how deeply you have invested in it,
Crossing the street of an event, as though coming out of it
     were
The same as making it happen. You're not sorry,
Of course, especially if this was the way it had to happen,
Yet would like an exacter share, something about time
That only a clock can tell you: how it feels, not what it
     means.
It is a long field, and we know only the far end of it,
Not the part we presumably had to go through to get there.
If it isn't enough, take the idea
Inherent in the day, armloads of wheat and flowers
Lying around flat on handtrucks, if maybe it means more
In pertaining to you, yet what is is what happens in the end
As though you cared. The event combined with

Beams leading up to it for the look of force adapted to the
    wiser
Usages of age, but it's both there
And not there, like washing or sawdust in the sunlight,
At the back of the mind, where we live now.

# Daffy Duck in Hollywood

Something strange is creeping across me.
La Celestina has only to warble the first few bars
Of "I Thought about You" or something mellow from
*Amadigi di Gaula* for everything—a mint-condition can
Of Rumford's Baking Powder, a celluloid earring, Speedy
Gonzales, the latest from Helen Topping Miller's fertile
Escritoire, a sheaf of suggestive pix on greige, deckle-edged
Stock—to come clattering through the rainbow trellis
Where Pistachio Avenue rams the 2300 block of Highland
Fling Terrace. He promised he'd get me out of this one,
That mean old cartoonist, but just look what he's
Done to me now! I scarce dare approach me mug's
    attenuated
Reflection in yon hubcap, so jaundiced, so *déconfit*
Are its lineaments—fun, no doubt, for some quack
    phrenologist's
Fern-clogged waiting room, but hardly what you'd call
Companionable. But everything is getting choked to the
    point of
Silence. Just now a magnetic storm hung in the swatch of sky
Over the Fudds' garage, reducing it—drastically—
To the aura of a plumbago-blue log cabin on
A Gadsden Purchase commemorative cover. Suddenly all is
Loathing. I don't want to go back inside any more. You
    meet
Enough vague people on this emerald traffic-island—no,

Not people, comings and goings, more: mutterings,
   splatterings,
The bizarrely but effectively equipped infantries of happy-
   go-nutty
Vegetal jacqueries, plumed, pointed at the little
White cardboard castle over the mill run. "Up
The lazy river, how happy we could be?"
How will it end? That geranium glow
Over Anaheim's had the riot act read to it by the
Etna-size firecracker that exploded last minute into
A *carte du Tendre* in whose lower right-hand corner
(Hard by the jock-itch sand-trap that skirts
The asparagus patch of algolagnic *nuits blanches*) Amadis
Is cozening the Princesse de Clèves into a midnight
   micturition spree
On the Tamigi with the Wallets (Walt, Blossom, and little
Skeezix) on a lamé barge "borrowed" from Ollie
Of the Movies' dread mistress of the robes. Wait!
I have an announcement! This wide, tepidly meandering,
Civilized Lethe (one can barely make out the maypoles
And *châlets de nécessité* on its sedgy shore) leads to Tophet,
   that
Landfill-haunted, not-so-residential resort from which
Some travellers return! This whole moment is the groin
Of a borborygmic giant who even now
Is rolling over on us in his sleep. Farewell bocages,
Tanneries, water-meadows. The allegory comes unsnarled
Too soon; a shower of pecky acajou harpoons is
About all there is to be noted between tornadoes. I have
Only my intermittent life in your thoughts to live
Which is like thinking in another language. Everything
Depends on whether somebody reminds you of me.
That this is a fabulation, and that those "other times"
Are in fact the silences of the soul, picked out in
Diamonds on stygian velvet, matters less than it should.

Prodigies of timing may be arranged to convince them
We live in one dimension, they in ours. While I
Abroad through all the coasts of dark destruction seek
Deliverance for us all, think in that language: its
Grammar, though tortured, offers pavilions
At each new parting of the ways. Pastel
Ambulances scoop up the quick and hie them to hospitals.
"It's all bits and pieces, spangles, patches, really; nothing
Stands alone. What happened to creative evolution?"
Sighed Aglavaine. Then to her Sélysette: "If his
Achievement is only to end up less boring than the others,
What's keeping us here? Why not leave at once?
I have to stay here while they sit in there,
Laugh, drink, have fine time. In my day
One lay under the tough green leaves,
Pretending not to notice how they bled into
The sky's aqua, the wafted-away no-color of regions
    supposed
Not to concern us. And so we too
Came where the others came: nights of physical endurance,
Or if, by day, our behavior was anarchically
Correct, at least by New Brutalism standards, all then
Grew taciturn by previous agreement. We were spirited
Away *en bateau*, under cover of fudge dark.
It's not the incomplete importunes, but the spookiness
Of the finished product. True, to ask less were folly, yet
If he is the result of himself, how much the better
For him we ought to be! And how little, finally,
We take this into account! Is the puckered garance satin
Of a case that once held a brace of dueling pistols our
Only acknowledging of that color? I like not this,
Methinks, yet this disappointing sequel to ourselves
Has been applauded in London and St. Petersburg. Somewhere
Ravens pray for us."
                   The storm finished brewing. And thus

She questioned all who came in at the great gate, but none
She found who ever heard of Amadis,
Nor of stern Aureng-Zebe, his first love. Some
There were to whom this mattered not a jot: since all
By definition is completeness (so
In utter darkness they reasoned), why not
Accept it as it pleases to reveal itself? As when
Low skyscrapers from lower-hanging clouds reveal
A turret there, an art-deco escarpment here, and last perhaps
The pattern that may carry the sense, but
Stays hidden in the mysteries of pagination.
Not what we see but how we see it matters; all's
Alike, the same, and we greet him who announces
The change as we would greet the change itself.
All life is but a figment; conversely, the tiny
Tome that slips from your hand is not perhaps the
Missing link in this invisible picnic whose leverage
Shrouds our sense of it. Therefore bivouac we
On this great, blond highway, unimpeded by
Veiled scruples, worn conundrums. Morning is
Impermanent. Grab sex things, swing up
Over the horizon like a boy
On a fishing expedition. No one really knows
Or cares whether this is the whole of which parts
Were vouchsafed—once—but to be ambling on's
The tradition more than the safekeeping of it. This mulch for
Play keeps them interested and busy while the big,
Vaguer stuff can decide what it wants—what maps, what
Model cities, how much waste space. Life, our
Life anyway, is between. We don't mind
Or notice any more that the sky *is* green, a parrot
One, but have our earnest where it chances on us,
Disingenuous, intrigued, inviting more,
Always invoking the echo, a summer's day.

# All Kinds of Caresses

The code-name losses and compensations
Float in and around us through the window.
It helps to know what direction the body comes from.
It isn't absolutely clear. In words
Bitter as a field of mustard we
Copy certain parts, then decline them.
These are not only gestures: they imply
Complex relations with one another. Sometimes one
Stays on for a while, a trace of lamp black
In a room full of gray furniture.

I now know all there is to know
About my body. I know too the direction
My feet are pointed in. For the time being
It is enough to suspend judgment, by which I don't mean
Forever, since judgment is also a storm, i.e., from
Somewhere else, sinking pleasure craft at moorings,
Looking, kicking in the sky.

Try to move with these hard blues,
These harsh yellows, these hands and feet.
Our gestures have taken us farther into the day
Than tomorrow will understand.

They live us. And we understand them when they sing,
Long after the perfume has worn off.
In the night the eye chisels a new phantom.

# Lost and Found and Lost Again

Like an object whose loss has begun to be felt
Though not yet noticed, your pulsar signals
To the present death. *"It must be cold out on the river
Today."* "You could make sweet ones on earth."

They tell him nothing. And the neon Bodoni
Presses its invitation to inspect the figures
Of this evening seeping from a far and fatal corridor
Of relaxed vigilance: these colors and this speech only.

# Two Deaths

The lace
Of spoken breathing fades quite quickly, becomes
Something it has no part in, the chairs and
The mugs used by the new young tenants, whose glance
Is elsewhere. The body rounds out the muted
Magic, and sighs.
             Unkind to want
To be here, but the way back is cut off:
You can only stand and nod, exchange stares, but
The time of manners is going, the woodpile in the corner
Of the lot exudes the peace of the forest. Perennially,
We die and are taken up again. How is it
With us, we are asked, and the voice
On the old Edison cylinder tells it: obliquity,
The condition of straightness of these tutorials,
Firm when it is held in the hand.

He goes out.
The empty parlor is as big as a hill.

# Houseboat Days

"The skin is broken. The hotel breakfast china
  Poking ahead to the last week in August, not really
  Very much at all, found the land where you began . . ."
The hills smouldered up blue that day, again
You walk five feet along the shore, and you duck
As a common heresy sweeps over. We can botanize
About this for centuries, and the little dazey
Blooms again in the cities. The mind
Is so hospitable, taking in everything
Like boarders, and you don't see until
It's all over how little there was to learn
Once the stench of knowledge has dissipated, and the
    trouvailles
Of every one of the senses fallen back. Really, he
Said, that insincerity of reasoning on behalf of one's
Sincere convictions, true or false in themselves
As the case may be, to which, if we are unwise enough
To argue at all with each other, we must be tempted
At times—do you see where it leads? To pain,
And the triumph over pain, still hidden
In these low-lying hills which rob us
Of all privacy, as though one were always about to meet
One's double through the chain of cigar smoke
And then it . . . happens, like an explosion in the brain,
Only it's a catastrophe on another planet to which
One has been invited, and as surely cannot refuse:

Pain in the cistern, in the gutters, and if we merely
Wait awhile, that denial, as though a universe of pain
Had been created just so as to deny its own existence.
But I don't set much stock in things
Beyond the weather and the certainties of living and dying:
The rest is optional. To praise this, blame that,
Leads one subtly away from the beginning, where
We must stay, in motion. To flash light
Into the house within, its many chambers,
Its memories and associations, upon its inscribed
And pictured walls, argues enough that life is various.
Life is beautiful. He who reads that
As in the window of some distant, speeding train
Knows what he wants, and what will befall.

Pinpricks of rain fall again.
And from across the quite wide median with its
Little white flowers, a reply is broadcast:
"Dissolve parliament. Hold new elections."
It would be deplorable if the rain also washed away
This profile at the window that moves, and moves on,
Knowing that it moves, and knows nothing else. It is the
    light
At the end of the tunnel as it might be seen
By him looking out somberly at the shower,
The picture of hope a dying man might turn away from,
Realizing that hope is something else, something concrete
You can't have. So, winding past certain pillars
Until you get to evening's malachite one, it becomes a vast
    dream
Of having that can topple governments, level towns and
    cities
With the pressure of sleep building up behind it.
The surge creates its own edge
And you must proceed this way: mornings of assent,

Indifferent noons leading to the ripple of the question
Of late afternoon projected into evening.
Arabesques and runnels are the result
Over the public address system, on the seismograph at
    Berkeley.
A little simple arithmetic tells you that to be with you
In this passage, this movement, is what the instance costs:
A sail out of some afternoon, like the clear dark blue
Eyes of Harold in Italy, beyond amazement, astonished,
Apparently not tampered with. As the rain gathers and
    protects
Its own darkness, the place in the slipcover is noticed
For the first and last time, fading like the spine
Of an adventure novel behind glass, behind the teacups.

# *Whether It Exists*

All through the fifties and sixties the land tilted
Toward the bowl of life. Now life
Has moved in that direction. We taste the conviction
Minus the rind, the pulp and the seeds. It
Goes down smoothly.

At a later date I added color
And the field became a shed in ways I no longer remember.
Familiarly, but without tenderness, the sunset pours its
Dance music on the (again) slanting barrens.
The problems we were speaking of move up toward them.

# The Lament upon the Waters

For the disciple nothing had changed. The mood was still
Gray tolerance, as the road marched along
Singing its little song of despair. Once, a cry
Started up out of the hills. That old, puzzling persuasion

Again. Sex was part of this,
And the shock of day turning into night.
Though we always found something delicate (too delicate
For some tastes, perhaps) to touch, to desire.

And we made much of this sort of materiality
That clogged the weight of starlight, made it seem
Fibrous, yet there was a chance in this
To see the present as it never had existed,

Clear and shapeless, in an atmosphere like cut glass.
At Latour-Maubourg you said this was a good thing, and
    on the steps
Of Métro Jasmin the couriers nodded to us correctly, and the
Pact was sealed in the sky. But now moments surround us

Like a crowd, some inquisitive faces, some hostile ones,
Some enigmatic or turned away to an anterior form of time
Given once and for all. The jetstream inscribes a final
    flourish
That melts as it stays. The problem isn't how to proceed

But is one of being: whether this ever was, and whose
It shall be. To be starting out, just one step
Off the sidewalk, and as such pulled back into the glittering
Snowstorm of stinging tentacles of how that would be
    worked out

If we ever work it out. And the voice came back at him
Across the water, rubbing it the wrong way: "Thou
Canst but undo the wrong thou hast done." The sackbuts
Embellish it, and we are never any closer to the collision

Of the waters, the peace of light drowning light,
Grabbing it, holding it up streaming. It is all one. It lies
All around, its new message, guilt, the admission
Of guilt, your new act. Time buys

The receiver, the onlooker of the earlier system, but cannot
Buy back the rest. It is night that fell
At the edge of your footsteps as the music stopped.
And we heard the bells for the first time. It is your chapter,
    I said.

# *Drame Bourgeois*

A sudden, acrid smell of roses, and the urchin
Turns away, tears level in the eyes. Waffled feeling:
"You'd scarce credit it, mum," as the starched
Moment of outline recedes down a corridor, some parts
Lighter, but the ensemble always darker as the vanishing
    point
Is reached and turns itself
Into an old army blanket, or something flat and material
As this idea of an old stump in a woods somewhere.
Then it is true. . . . It is you, who, that
Wet evening in March . . . Madam, say no more,
Your very lack of information is special to me,
Your emptying glance, prisms which I treasure up.
Only let your voice not become this clarion,
Alarum in the wilderness, calling me back to piety, to sense,
Else I am undone, for late haze drapes the golf links
And the gilded spines of these tomes blaze too bright.

# *And* Ut Pictura Poesis *Is Her Name*

You can't say it that way any more.
Bothered about beauty you have to
Come out into the open, into a clearing,
And rest. Certainly whatever funny happens to you
Is OK. To demand more than this would be strange
Of you, you who have so many lovers,
People who look up to you and are willing
To do things for you, but you think
It's not right, that if they really knew you . . .
So much for self-analysis. Now,
About what to put in your poem-painting:
Flowers are always nice, particularly delphinium.
Names of boys you once knew and their sleds,
Skyrockets are good—do they still exist?
There are a lot of other things of the same quality
As those I've mentioned. Now one must
Find a few important words, and a lot of low-keyed,
Dull-sounding ones. She approached me
About buying her desk. Suddenly the street was
Bananas and the clangor of Japanese instruments.
Humdrum testaments were scattered around. His head
Locked into mine. We were a seesaw. Something
Ought to be written about how this affects
You when you write poetry:
The extreme austerity of an almost empty mind

Colliding with the lush, Rousseau-like foliage of its desire to
    communicate
Something between breaths, if only for the sake
Of others and their desire to understand you and desert you
For other centers of communication, so that understanding
May begin, and in doing so be undone.

So that communication
begin it so become undone.

# What Is Poetry

The medieval town, with frieze
Of boy scouts from Nagoya? The snow

That came when we wanted it to snow?
Beautiful images? Trying to avoid

Ideas, as in this poem? But we
Go back to them as to a wife, leaving

The mistress we desire? Now they
Will have to believe it

As we believe it. In school
All the thought got combed out:

What was left was like a field.
Shut your eyes, and you can feel it for miles around.

Now open them on a thin vertical path.
It might give us—what?—some flowers soon?

# And Others, Vaguer Presences

Are built out of the meshing of life and space
At the point where we are wholly revealed
In the lozenge-shaped openings. Because
It is argued that these structures address themselves
To exclusively aesthetic concerns, like windmills
On a vast plain. To which it is answered
That there are no other questions than these,
Half squashed in mud, emerging out of the moment
We all live, learning to like it. No sonnet
On this furthest strip of land, no pebbles,

No plants. To extend one's life
All day on the dirty stone of some plaza,
Unaware among the pretty lunging of the wind,
Light and shade, is like coming out of
A coma that is a white, interesting country,
Prepared to lose the main memory in a meeting
By torchlight under the twisted end of the stairs.

# The Wrong Kind of Insurance

I teach in a high school
And see the nurses in some of the hospitals,
And if all teachers are like that
Maybe I can give you a buzz some day,
Maybe we can get together for lunch or coffee or something.

The white marble statues in the auditorium
Are colder to the touch than the rain that falls
Past the post-office inscription about rain or snow
Or gloom of night. I think
About what these archaic meanings mean,
That unfurl like a rope ladder down through history,
To fall at our feet like crocuses.

All of our lives is a rebus
Of little wooden animals painted shy,
Terrific colors, magnificent and horrible,
Close together. The message is learned
The way light at the edge of a beach in autumn is learned.
The seasons are superimposed.
In New York we have winter in August
As they do in Argentina and Australia.
Spring is leafy and cold, autumn pale and dry.
And changes build up
Forever, like birds released into the light
Of an August sky, falling away forever

To define the handful of things we know for sure,
Followed by musical evenings.

Yes, friends, these clouds pulled along on invisible ropes
Are, as you have guessed, merely stage machinery,
And the funny thing is it knows we know
About it and still wants us to go on believing
In what it so unskillfully imitates, and wants
To be loved not for that but for itself:
The murky atmosphere of a park, tattered
Foliage, wise old treetrunks, rainbow tissue-paper wadded
Clouds down near where the perspective
Intersects the sunset, so we may know
We too are somehow impossible, formed of so many
    different things,
Too many to make sense to anybody.
We straggle on as quotients, hard-to-combine
Ingredients, and what continues
Does so with our participation and consent.

Try milk of tears, but it is not the same.
The dandelions will have to know why, and your comic
Dirge routine will be lost on the unfolding sheaves
Of the wind, a lucky one, though it will carry you
Too far, to some manageable, cold, open
Shore of sorrows you expected to reach,
Then leave behind.
                Thus, friend, this distilled,
Dispersed musk of moving around, the product
Of leaf after transparent leaf, of too many
Comings and goings, visitors at all hours.
                      Each night
Is trifoliate, strange to the touch.

# The Serious Doll

The kinds of thing are more important than the
Individual thing, though the specific is supremely
Interesting. Right? As each particular
Goes over Niagara Falls in a barrel one may
Justifiably ask: Where does this come from?
Whither goes my concern? What you are wearing
Has vanished along with other concepts.
They are lined up by the factory balcony railing
Against blue sky with some clumsy white paper clouds
Pasted on it. Where does the east meet the west?
At sunset there is a choice of two smiles: discreet or serious.
In this best of all possible worlds, that is enough.

# *Friends*

*I like to speak in rhymes,*
*because I am a rhyme myself.*

Nijinsky

I saw a cottage in the sky.
I saw a balloon made of lead.
*I cannot restrain my tears, and they fall*
*On my left hand and on my silken tie,*
*But I cannot and do not want to hold them back.*

One day the neighbors complain about an unpleasant odor
Coming from his room. *I went for a walk*
*But met no friends.* Another time I go outside
Into the world. It rocks on and on.
It was rocking before I saw it
And is presumably doing so still.

The banker lays his hand on mine.
His face is as clean as a white handkerchief.
We talk nonsense as usual.
I trace little circles on the light that comes in
Through the window on saw-horse legs.
Afterwards I see that we are three.
Someone had entered the room while I was discussing my
    money problems.
I wish God would put a stop to this. I
Turn and see the new moon through glass. I am yanked
    away
So fast I lose my breath, a not unpleasant feeling.

I feel as though I had been carrying the message for years
On my shoulders like Atlas, never feeling it
Because of never having known anything else. In another
   way
I am involved with the message. I want to put it down
(In two senses of "put it down") so that you
May understand the agreeable destiny that awaits us.
You sigh. Your sighs will admit of no impatience,
Only a vast crater lake, vast as the sea,
In which the sky, smaller than that, is reflected.

I reach for my hat
And am bound to repeat with tact
The formal greeting I am charged with.
No one makes mistakes. No one runs away
Any more. I bite my lip and
Turn to you. Maybe now you understand.

The feeling is a jewel like a pearl.

# The Thief of Poetry

To you
my friend who
was in this

street once
were on it
getting

in with it
getting on with it
though

only passing by
a smell of hamburgers
that day

an old mattress
and a box spring
as it

darkened
filling the empty
rumble

of a street
in decay of time
it fell out that

there was no
remaining
whether out of a wish

to be moving on
or frustrated
willingness to stay

here to stand
still
the moment

had other plans
and now in this
jungle of darkness

the future still makes plans
O ready to go
Conceive of your plight

more integrally
the snow
that day

buried all but the most obtuse
only the most generalized
survives

the low profile
becomes a constant again
the line of ocean

of shore
nestling
confident

impermanent
to rise again
in new

vicissitude
in explicit
triumph

drowns the hum
of space
the false point

of the stars
in specific
new way of happening

Now
no one remembers
the day you walked a certain distance

along the beach
and then
walked back

it seems
in your tracks
because it

was ending
for the first time
yes but now

is another way of
spreading out
toward the end

the linear style
is discarded
though this is

not realized for centuries
meanwhile
another way of living had come and gone

leaving its width
behind
now the tall cedars

had become locked into
the plan
so that everywhere

you looked
was burning
inferential

interior space
not for colonies
but already closed

turned in on itself
its back
as beautiful as the sea

where you go up
and say the word
eminence

to yourself
all was lived in
had been lived in

was coming to an end
again
in the featureless present

that was expanding to
cloister it
this just a little too

comic parable
and so insure the second
beginning

of that day seen against the street
of whichever way
you walked and talked

knowing not knowing
the thing that was describing you
and not knowing

your taller
well somehow more informed
bearing

as you wind down
only a second
it did matter

you come back so seldom
but it's all right
the way of staying

you started comes back
procession into the fire
into the sky

the dream you lost
firm in its day
reassured and remembered

# The Ice-Cream Wars

Although I mean it, and project the meaning
As hard as I can into its brushed-metal surface,
It cannot, in this deteriorating climate, pick up
Where I leave off. It sees the Japanese text
(About two men making love on a foam-rubber bed)
As among the most massive secretions of the human spirit.
Its part is in the shade, beyond the iron spikes of the fence,
Mixing red with blue. As the day wears on
Those who come to seem reasonable are shouted down
(*Why you old goat!* Look who's talkin'. Let's see you
Climb off that tower—the waterworks architecture, both
    stupid and
Grandly humorous at the same time, is a kind of mask for
    him,
Like a seal's face. Time and the weather
Don't always go hand in hand, as here: sometimes
One is slanted sideways, disappears for awhile.
Then later it's forget-me-not time, and rapturous
Clouds appear above the lawn, and the rose tells
The old old story, the pearl of the orient, occluded
And still apt to rise at times.)
                              A few black smudges
On the outer boulevards, like squashed midges
And the truth becomes a hole, something one has always
    known,

A heaviness in the trees, and no one can say
Where it comes from, or how long it will stay—

A randomness, a darkness of one's own.

# *Valentine*

Like a serpent among roses, like an asp
Among withered thornapples I coil to
And at you. The name of the castle is you,
*El Rey*. It is an all-night truck-stop
Offering the best coffee and hamburgers in Utah.
It is most beautiful and nocturnal by daylight.
Seven layers: moss-agate, coral, aventurine,
Carnelian, Swiss lapis, obsidian—maybe others.
You know now that it has the form of a string
Quartet. The different parts are always meddling with each
    other,
Pestering each other, getting in each other's way
So as to withdraw skillfully at the end, leaving—what?
A new kind of emptiness, maybe bathed in freshness,
Maybe not. Maybe just a new kind of emptiness.

You are smart but the weather of this day startles and japes
at you. You come out of it in pieces. Always pursuing you
is the knowledge that I am there unable to turn around, un-
able to confront you with your otherness. This is another
one of my houses, the one in Hampstead, the brick one in
the middle of the block that you never saw though you
passed along that street many times, sometimes in spring
with a light drizzle blowing that made you avert your gaze,
sometimes at the height of summer where the grandeur of
the ideas of the trees swamped your ideas about everything,

so you never saw my house. It was near where Arthur Rackham lived. I can't quite remember the name of the street—some partly legible inscription on a Victorian urn: E and then MEL(E?), perhaps a Latin exhortation to apples or heroism, and down in the dim part a name like "Rossiter," but that is too far down. Listen, I never meant for you not to be in my house. But you couldn't because you were it.

In this part I reflect on the difficulty and surprise of being you. It may never get written. Some things are simultaneously too boring and too exciting to write about. This has to be one of them. Some day, when we're stoned . . . Meanwhile, write to me. I enjoy and appreciate your phone calls, but it's nice to get cards and letters too—so keep 'em comin'!

Through bearded twilight I hear things like "Now see here, young man!" or "Henry Groggins, you old reprobate!" or "For an hour Lester has been staring at budget figures, making no progress." I know these things are, that they are. At night there are a few things, and they slide along to make room for others. Seen through an oval frame, one of the walls of a parlor. The wallpaper is a conventionalized pattern, the sliced okra and star-anise one, held together with crudely gummed links of different colored paper, among which purple predominates, stamped over a flocked background of grisaille shepherdesses and dogs urinating against fire hydrants. To reflect on the consummate skill with which the artist has rendered the drops as they bounce off the hydrant and collect in a gleaming sun-yellow pool below the curb is a sobering experience. Only the shelf of the mantelpiece shows. At each end, seated on pedestals turned slightly away from one another, two aristocratic bisque figures, a boy in delicate cerise and a girl in cornflower blue. Their shadows join in a grotesque silhouette. In the center, an ancient clock whose tick acts as the metronome for the sound of their high voices. Presently the mouths of the figures open and shut, after the mode of ordinary conversation.


Thought I'd
Row across to you this afternoon,
My Irina! Always writing your beloved articles,
I see. Happened on one only recently in one of the more
    progressive journals.
Brilliantly written, or so it seemed, but isn't your thought
    a bit too
Advanced by present-day standards? Of course, there was
    much truth
In what you said, but don't you feel the public sometimes
    has more truth
Than it can cope with? I don't mean that you should . . .
    well, "fib,"
But perhaps, well, heh heh, temper the wind to the shorn
    lamb
A bit. Eh? How about it, old boy?
Or are you so in love with your "advanced" thinking that
    everything else
Seems old hat to you, including my conversation no doubt?
    In that
Case I ought to be getting on. Goodness, I've a four-thirty
    appointment and it's
Already five after. What have you done with my hat?


These things I write for you and you only.
Do not judge them too harshly. Temper the wind,
As he was saying. They are infant things
That may grow up to be children, perhaps—who knows?—
Even adults some day, but now they exist only in the
    blindness
Of your love for me and are the proof of it.

You can't think about them too long
Without knocking them over. Your castle is a house of cards,
The old-fashioned kind of playing cards, towering farther
Than the eye can see into the clouds, and it is also built on
Shifting sands, its base slurps out of sight too. I am the
    inhabitable one.
But my back is as a door to you, now open, now shut,
And your kisses are as dreams, or an elixir
Of radium, or flowers of some kind.
Remember about what I told you.

# Blue Sonata

Long ago was the then beginning to seem like now
As now is but the setting out on a new but still
Undefined way. *That* now, the one once
Seen from far away, is our destiny
No matter what else may happen to us. It is
The present past of which our features,
Our opinions are made. We are half it and we
Care nothing about the rest of it. We
Can see far enough ahead for the rest of us to be
Implicit in the surroundings that twilight is.
We know that this part of the day comes every day
And we feel that, as it has its rights, so
We have our right to be ourselves in the measure
That we are in it and not some other day, or in
Some other place. The time suits us
Just as it fancies itself, but just so far
As we not give up that inch, breath
Of becoming before becoming may be seen,
Or come to seem all that it seems to mean now.

The things that were coming to be talked about
Have come and gone and are still remembered
As being recent. There is a grain of curiosity
At the base of some new thing, that unrolls
Its question mark like a new wave on the shore.
In coming to give, to give up what we had,

We have, we understand, gained or been gained
By what was passing through, bright with the sheen
Of things recently forgotten and revived.
Each image fits into place, with the calm
Of not having too many, of having just enough.
We live in the sigh of our present.

If that was all there was to have
We could re-imagine the other half, deducing it
From the shape of what is seen, thus
Being inserted into its idea of how we
Ought to proceed. It would be tragic to fit
Into the space created by our not having arrived yet,
To utter the speech that belongs there,
For progress occurs through re-inventing
These words from a dim recollection of them,
In violating that space in such a way as
To leave it intact. Yet we do after all
Belong here, and have moved a considerable
Distance; our passing is a facade.
But our understanding of it is justified.

# Spring Light

The buildings, piled so casually
Behind each other, are "suggestions
Which, while only suggestions,
We hope you will take seriously." Off into
The blue. Getting there is easier,
But then we hope you will come down.
There is a great deal on the ground today,
Not just mud, but things of some importance,
Too. Like, silver paint. How do you feel
About it? And, is this a silver age?
Yeah. I suppose so. But I keep looking at the cigarette
Burns on the edge of the sink, left over
From last winter. Your argument's
Neatly beyond any paths I'm likely to take,
Here, or when I eventually leave here.

# Syringa

Orpheus liked the glad personal quality
Of the things beneath the sky. Of course, Eurydice was a part
Of this. Then one day, everything changed. He rends
Rocks into fissures with lament. Gullies, hummocks
Can't withstand it. The sky shudders from one horizon
To the other, almost ready to give up wholeness.
Then Apollo quietly told him: "Leave it all on earth.
Your lute, what point? Why pick at a dull pavan few care to
Follow, except a few birds of dusty feather,
Not vivid performances of the past." But why not?
All other things must change too.
The seasons are no longer what they once were,
But it is the nature of things to be seen only once,
As they happen along, bumping into other things, getting
     along
Somehow. That's where Orpheus made his mistake.
Of course Eurydice vanished into the shade;
She would have even if he hadn't turned around.
No use standing there like a gray stone toga as the whole
     wheel
Of recorded history flashes past, struck dumb, unable to
     utter an intelligent
Comment on the most thought-provoking element in its
     train.
Only love stays on the brain, and something these people,
These other ones, call life. Singing accurately

So that the notes mount straight up out of the well of
Dim noon and rival the tiny, sparkling yellow flowers
Growing around the brink of the quarry, encapsulizes
The different weights of the things.

                              But it isn't enough
To just go on singing. Orpheus realized this
And didn't mind so much about his reward being in heaven
After the Bacchantes had torn him apart, driven
Half out of their minds by his music, what it was doing to
    them.
Some say it was for his treatment of Eurydice.
But probably the music had more to do with it, and
The way music passes, emblematic
Of life and how you cannot isolate a note of it
And say it is good or bad. You must
Wait till it's over. "The end crowns all,"
Meaning also that the "tableau"
Is wrong. For although memories, of a season, for example,
Melt into a single snapshot, one cannot guard, treasure
That stalled moment. It too is flowing, fleeting;
It is a picture of flowing, scenery, though living, mortal,
Over which an abstact action is laid out in blunt,
Harsh strokes. And to ask more than this
Is to become the tossing reeds of that slow,
Powerful stream, the trailing grasses
Playfully tugged at, but to participate in the action
No more than this. Then in the lowering gentian sky
Electric twitches are faintly apparent first, then burst forth
Into a shower of fixed, cream-colored flares. The horses
Have each seen a share of the truth, though each thinks,
"I'm a maverick. Nothing of this is happening to me,
Though I can understand the language of birds, and
The itinerary of the lights caught in the storm is fully
    apparent to me.
Their jousting ends in music much

As trees move more easily in the wind after a summer storm
And is happening in lacy shadows of shore-trees, now, day
   after day."

But how late to be regretting all this, even
Bearing in mind that regrets are always late, too late!
To which Orpheus, a bluish cloud with white contours,
Replies that these are of course not regrets at all,
Merely a careful, scholarly setting down of
Unquestioned facts, a record of pebbles along the way.
And no matter how all this disappeared,
Or got where it was going, it is no longer
Material for a poem. Its subject
Matters too much, and not enough, standing there helplessly
While the poem streaked by, its tail afire, a bad
Comet screaming hate and disaster, but so turned inward
That the meaning, good or other, can never
Become known. The singer thinks
Constructively, builds up his chant in progressive stages
Like a skyscraper, but at the last minute turns away.
The song is engulfed in an instant in blackness
Which must in turn flood the whole continent
With blackness, for it cannot see. The singer
Must then pass out of sight, not even relieved
Of the evil burthen of the words. Stellification
Is for the few, and comes about much later
When all record of these people and their lives
Has disappeared into libraries, onto microfilm.
A few are still interested in them. "But what about
So-and-so?" is still asked on occasion. But they lie
Frozen and out of touch until an arbitrary chorus
Speaks of a totally different incident with a similar name
In whose tale are hidden syllables
Of what happened so long before that
In some small town, one indifferent summer.

# Fantasia on "The Nut-Brown Maid"

HE

Be it right or wrong, these men among
Others in the park, all those years in the cold,
Are a plain kind of thing: bands
Of acanthus and figpeckers. At
The afternoon closing you walk out
Of the dream crowding the walls and out
Of life or whatever filled up
Those days and seemed to be life.
You borrowed its colors, the drab ones
That are so popular now, though only
For a minute, and extracted a fashion
That wasn't really there. You are
Going, I from your thought rapidly
To the green wood go, alone, a banished man.

SHE

But now always from your plaint I
Relive, revive, springing up careless,
Dust geyser in city absentmindedness,
And all day it is writ and said:
We round women like corners. They are the friends
We are always saying goodbye to and then
Bumping into the next day. School has closed
Its doors on a few. Saddened, she rose up

And untwined the gears of that blank, blossoming day.
"So much for Paris, and the living in this world."
But I was going to say
It differently, about the way
Time is sorting us all out, keeping you and her
Together yet apart, in a give-and-take, push-pull
Kind of environment. And then, packed like sardines,
Our wit arises, survives automatically. We imbibe it.

HE

What was all the manner
Between them, let us discuss, the sponge
Of night pick us up with much else, carry
Some distance, so all the pain and fear
Will never be heard by anybody. Gasping
On your porch, but I look to new season
Which is exactly lost. "I am the knight,
I come by night." We will say all these
To the other, in turn. And now impatient for
Sleep will have strayed over the
Frontier to pass the time, and it might
As well, dried baby's breath stuck in an old
Bottle, and no man puts out to sea from these
Coves, secure or not, dwelling in persuasion.

SHE

It's as I thought: there there is
Nothing solid, nothing one can build on. The
Force may have ebbed in the green wood.
Here is nothing, not even
Lazy slipping away, feeling of being abandoned, a
Distant curl of smoke above a car
Graveyard. Instead, the shadows stand
Straight out. Uninvited, light grabs its due;

What is eaten away becomes etched impression
Of mutability, but nothing backs it up.
We may as well begin the litany here:
How all that forgotten past seasons us, prepares
Us for each other, now that the mathematics
Of winter is starting to point it out.

HE

It is true, a truer story.
Self-knowledge frosts each action, each step taken
Freely. Life is a living picture.
Alone, I can bind you like a pleated scarf
But beyond that is much that might be
Examined for the purpose of examining it.
The ends stream back in the wind, it is too dark
To see them but I can feel them.
As Naming-of-Cares you precede the objection
To each, implying a Land of Cockaigne
Syndrome. You get around this as though
The eternally revised geography of spring meant
Something beyond its own sense of exaltation,
And love were cause for self-congratulation.

SHE

I might hide somewhere. I want to fly but keep
My morality, motley as it is, just by
Encouraging these branching diversions around an axis.
So when suddenly a cloud blackens the whole
Day just before noon, this is merely
Timing. So even when darkness swings further
Back, it indicates, must indicate, an order,
Albeit a restricted one, which tends to prove that idle
Civilizations once existed under a loose heading like
"The living and the dead." To learn more

Isn't my way, and anyway the dark green
Ring around the basin postulates
More than the final chapter of this intriguing
Unfinished last chapter. It's in the public domain.

HE

But you will take comfort in it again.
Others, patient murderers, cultivated,
Sympathetic, in time will have subtly
Switched the background from parallel rain-lines
To the ambiguities of "the deep," and in
Doing so will have wheeled an equestrian statue up
Against the sky's facade, the eye of God, cantering
So as not to fall back nor yet trample the cold
Pourings of sunlight. You will have the look
Reflected on your face. The great squash domes seem
To vindicate us all, yet belong to no one.
Meanwhile others will grow up and fuck and
Get older, beating like weeds against the door,
But this wasn't anticipated. You caught them off guard.

SHE

What I hear scraping at the door
Is palaver of multitudes who decided to come back,
Having set out too soon, and something must be
Done about them, names must be written down,
Or simply by being hoarse one whole side
Of the world won't count any more,
The side with the story of our lives
And our relatives' on it, the memory
Of the day you bicycled over.
But the reason for the even, tawny flow
Of the morning as it turned was the thought of riding
Back down all those hills that were so hard

To get up, and climbing the ones you had
Coasted down before, like mirror-writing.


HE

And when the flourish under the signature,
A miniature beehive with a large bee on it, was
Finished, you chose a view of distant factories,
Tall smokestacks, anything. It didn't matter
So long as it was emptied of all but a drop
At the bottom like the medicine bottle that is thrown away.
The catch in the voice goes out of style then,
The period of civilities is long past.
Strange we should be continually waking up
To a barbaric calm that has probably
Always supported us, while still
Apologizing to the off-white walls we saw through
Years ago. But it stays this way.


SHE

What happened was you had finished
Nine-tenths of it before the great explosion,
The meteorite or whatever it was that tore out the
Huge crater eight miles in diameter.
Then somehow you spliced the bleeding wires,
Made it presentable long enough for
Inspection, then collapsed and slept until
The part where she takes the bus. And all
Because someone in a department store made some
Cryptic allusion, or so you thought as that person
Passed by, reducing the architecture of a life
To a minus quantity. There was no way
Back out of this because it wasn't a departure.

## HE

I once stole a pencil, but now the list with my name in it
Disgusts me. It is the horizon, tilted like the deck
Of a ship. And beyond, what must be the real
Horizon congeals into a blue roebuck whose shadow
Hardens every upturned face it trails across
And sets a blister there. If there was still time
To turn back, you must not follow me, but rather
Stay in your living, in your time,
Sizing up the future as accurately as the woman
In the old photograph, and, like her, turn away,
Your hand barely grazing the top of the little doric column.
Anything outside what the sheaf of rays delineates
For the moment is pain and at least illusion,
A piece of not very good news.

## SHE

Then we must be like each other, because this afternoon's
Ballast barely holds back the rising landscape
Of premonitions against that now distant (yet all too
Contemporaneous) magnesium flare in which
The habits of a moment, like wrinkles in a piece of
    backcloth,
Plummeted into the space under the stage
Through a trapdoor carelessly left open,
Joining other manifestations of human stick-to-itiveness
In a "semi-retirement" which has its own rewards
Except the solution only comes about much later, and then
Won't entirely fit all the clues of the atmosphere
(Books, dishes and bathrooms), but is
Empty and vigilant, but too late to make the train,
And at night stands like tall buildings, disembodied,
Vaporous, rhapsodic, going on and on about something
That happened in the past, at the point where the recent
Past ends and the darker one begins.

But since "we know what we are, but know not
What we may be," and it's later now, the romance
Of moderation takes over again. Something has to be
Living, not everyone can afford the luxury of
Just being, not alive but being, at the center,
The perfumed, patterned center. Perhaps it's all fun
But we won't know till we see it, as on a windless day
It suddenly becomes obvious how wonderful the fields are
Before it all sickens and fades to a melange
Of half-truths, this gray dump. Then double trouble
Arrives, Beppo and Zeppo confront one
Out of a hurricane of colored dots, twin
Windshield wipers dealing the accessories:
Woe, wrack, wet—probably another kingdom.

I was going to say that the sky
Could never become that totally self-absorbed, bachelor's-
Button blue, yet it has, and nothing is any safer for it,
Though the outlines of what we did stay just a second longer
On the etching of the forest, and we know enough not
To go there. If brimstone were the same as the truth
A gate deep in the ground would unlock to the fumbling
Of a certain key and the dogs at the dog races
Would circumambulate each in his allotted groove
Casting an exaggeratedly long shadow, while other
Malcontents, troublemakers, *esprits frondeurs* moved up
To dissolve in the brightness of the footlights. I would
Withstand, bow in hand, to grieve them. So it is time
To wake up, to commingle with the little walking presences, all
Somehow related, to each other and through each other to us,
Characters in the opera *The Flood*, by the great anonymous
    composer.

## HE

Mostly they are
Shoals, even tricks of the light, armies
In debacle, helter skelter, pell mell,
Fleeing us who sometime did us seek,
And there is no place, nothing
To hide in, if it took weeks and months
With time running out. Nothing could be done.
Those ramparts, granular as Saturn's rings,
That seem some tomb of pleasures, a Sans Souci,
Are absent clouds. The real diversions on the ground
Are shrub and nettle, planing the way
For asking me to come down, and the snow, the frost, the
    rain,
The cold, the heat, for dry or wet
We must lodge on the plain. . . . Later, dying
"Of complications," only it must really have been much
    later, her hair
Had that whited look. Now it's darker.

## SHE

And an intruder is present.
But it always winds down like this
To the rut of night. Boats no longer come
Plying along the sides of docks in this part
Of the world. We are alone. Only by climbing
A low bluff does the intent get filled in
Along the edge, and then only subtly.
Evening weaves along these open tracts almost
Until the solemn tolling of a bell
Launches its moment of pain and obscurity, wider
Than any net can seize, or star presage. Further on it says
That all the missing parts must be tracked down
By coal-light or igloo-light because

79

In so doing we navigate these our passages,
And take sides on certain issues, are
Emphatically pro or con about what concerns us,
Such as the strangeness of our architecture,
The diffuse quality of our literature.


HE

Or does each tense fit, and each desire
Drown in the lake of one vague one, featureless
And indeterminate? Which is why one's own wish
Keeps getting granted for someone else? In the forest
Are no clean sheets, no other house
But leaves and boughs. How many
Other things can one want? Nice hair
And eyes, galoshes on a rainy day? For those who go
Under the green helm know it lets itself
Become known, at different moments, under different
    aspects.


SHE

Unless some movie did it first, or
A stranger came to the door and then the change
Was real until it went away. Or is it
Like a landscape in its inner folds, relaxed
And with the sense of there being about to be some more
Until the first part is digested and then it twists
Only because this is the way we can see things?
It is revisionism in that you are
Always trying to put some part of the past back in,
And although it fits it doesn't belong in the
Dark blue glass ocean of having been remembered again.
From earliest times we were cautioned not to get excited
About things, so this quality shows up so far only in

Slightly deeper tree-shadows that anticipate this PACING
  THE FLOOR
That takes in the walls, the window and the woods.

HE

Then it was as if a kind of embarrassment,
The product of a discretion lodged far back in the past,
Blotted them against a wall of haze.
Pursuing time this way, as a dog nudges a bone,
You find it has doubled back, the flanges
Of night having now replaced the big daffy gray clouds.
O now no longer speak, but rather seem
In the way of gardens long ago turned away from,
And now no one any more will have to believe anything
He or she doesn't want to as golden light wholly
Saturates a wooden fence and speaks for everybody
In a native accent that sounds new and foreign.
But the hesitation stayed on, and came to be permanent
Because they were thinking about each other.

SHE

That's an unusual . . . As though a new crescent
Reached out and lapped at a succession of multitudes,
Diminished now, but still lively and true.
It seems to say: there are lots of differences inside.
There were differences when only you knew them.
Now they are an element, not themselves,
And hands are idle, or weigh the head
Like an outsize grapefruit, or an ocarina
Closes today with a comical wail.
Go in to them, see
What the session was about, how much they destroyed
And what preserved of what was meant to shuffle

Along in its time: hunched red shoulders
Of huntsmen, what they were doing
There in the grass, ribbons of time fluttering
From the four corners of a square masonry tower.

### HE

Having draped ourselves in villas, across verandas
For so many years, having sampled
Rose petals and newspapers, we know that the eye of the
    storm,
As it moves majestically to engulf us, is alive
With the spirit of confusion, and that these birds
Are stamped with the same dream of exaltation moving
Toward the end. 'Tis said of old, soon
Hot, soon cold. There are other kinds of privacy
Coming in now, and soon,
In three or four months, enough leisure
To examine the claim of each
And to reward each according to his claim
On a sliding scale coinciding with the rush
Into later blue sun-divided weather.

### SHE

No, but I dug these out of bureau drawers for you,
Told you which ones meant a lot to me,
Which ones I was frankly dubious about, and
Which were destined to blow away.
Who are we to suffer after this?
The fragrant cunt, the stubborn penis, winding
Paths of despair and memory, reproach in
The stairwell, and new confidence: "We'll
Do something about that," until a later date
When pines march stiffly right down to the edge of the
    water.

And after all this, finding
Someone at home, as though memory
Had placed chairs around
So that these seem to come and go in the present
And will escape the anger of a fixed
falling back to the vase again like a fountain. Responsible
Destiny causing them to lean all the way over to one side
Like wind-heaped foam.

HE

It's enough that they are had,
Allowed to run loose.
As I was walking all alane
The idea of a field of particulars—that
Each is shaped, illustratable, accountable
To us and to no man—leached into the pervading
Gray-blue sense of moving somewhere with coevals,
Palmers and pardoners, a raucous yet erasable
Rout pent in the glimmer of
An American Bar. Whereupon Barry Sullivan-type avers
To Bruce Bennett-type that inert wet blackness is
Superior to boudoir light in which
Dull separateness blazes and is shriven and
Knows it isn't right.

SHE

And shall, like a Moebius strip
Of a tapestry, play to our absences and soothe them,
Whether in some deprived tropic or some
Boudoir-cave where it finds that just
Paying the interest on the bonanza is dressier.
*Alas, but there are others*, he thought, and we are children
Again, the children our parents were, trampling
Under foot the delicate boundary, last thing of day

*83*

Before night, that resurrects and comforts us here. Patience
Of articulation between us is still what it is,
No more and no less, but this time the night shift
Will have to be disturbed, and wiping out the quality
Of yesterday with the sponge of dreams is being phased out.

HE

You're making a big mistake. Just because Goofus has been
lucky for you, you imagine others will make a fuss over you,
all the others, who will matriculate. You'll be left with a
trowel and a lot of empty flowerpots, imagining that the
sun as it enters this window is somehow a blessing that will
make up for everything else—those very years in the cold.
That the running faucet is a sacred stream. That the glint of
light from a silver ball on that far-off flagpole is the equiva-
lent of a career devoted to life, to improving the minds and
the welfare of others, when in reality it is a common thing
like these, and less profitable than any hobby or sideline that
is a source of retirement income, such as an antique stall,
pecan harvest or root-beer stand. In short, although the
broad outlines of your intentions are a credit to you, what
fills them up isn't. You are like someone whose face was
photographed in a crowd scene once and then gradually re-
treated from people's memories, and from life as well.

SHE

But the real "world"
Stretches its pretending into the side yard
Where I was waiting, at peace with my feelings, though
    now,
I see, resentful from the beginning for the change to happen
Like lilacs. We were walking
All along toward a door that seemed to recede
In the distance and now is somehow behind us, shut,

Though apparently it didn't lock automatically. How
Wonderful the fields are. They are
Like love poetry, all the automatic breathing going on
All around, and there are enchanted, many-colored
Things like houses to explore, if there were time,
But the house is built under a waterfall. The slanting
Roof and the walls are made of opaque glass, and
The emerald-green wall-to-wall carpeting is sopping moss.

HE

And last, perhaps, as darkness
Begins to infuse the lawns and silent streets
And the remote estuary, and thickens here, you mention
The slamming of a door I wasn't supposed to know about,
That took years. Each of us circles
Around some simple but vital missing piece of information,
And, at the end, as now, finding no substitute,
Writes his own mark grotesquely with a stick in snow,
The signature of many connected seconds of indecision.
What I am writing to say is, the timing, not
The contents, is what matters. All this could have happened
Long ago, or at least on some other day,
And not meant much except insofar as the eye
Extracts a progress from almost anything. But then
It wouldn't have become a toy.
And all the myths,
Legends and misinterpretations, would have scattered
At a single pistol shot. And it would no longer know what
    I know.

SHE

It was arriving now, the eyes thick
With their black music, the wooden misquotable side
Thrust forward. Tell about the affair she'd had

With Bennett Palmer, the Minnesota highwayman,
Back when she was staying at Lake Geneva, Wisc.,
In the early forties. That paynim'd
Go to any lengths to shut her up, now,
Now that the time of truth telling from tall towers
Had come. Only old Thomas a Tattamus with his two tups
Seemed really to care. Even Ellen herself
Could muster but a few weak saws about loving—how it
    leaves us
Naked at a time when we would rather be clothed, and
She looked all around the room with a satisfied air.
Everything was in order, even unto bareness, waiting to
    receive
Whatever stamp or seal. The light coming in off the kale
In the kaleyard outside was like the joyous, ravening
Light over the ocean the morning after a storm.
It hadn't betrayed her and it never would.


HE

To him, the holiday-making crowds were
Engines of a parallel disaster, the fulfilling
Of all prophecies between now and the day of
Judgment. Spiralling like fish,
Toward a distant, unperceived surface, was all
The reflection there was. Somewhere it had its opaque
Momentary existence.
                    But if each act
Is reflexive, concerned with itself on another level
As well as with us, the strangers who live here,
Can one advance one step further without sinking equally
Far back into the past? There was always something to see,
Something going on, for the historical past owed it
To itself, our historical present. Another month a huge
Used-car sale on the lawn shredded the sense of much

Of the sun coming through the wires, or a cape
Would be rounded by a slim white sail almost
Invisible in the specific design, or children would come
Clattering down fire escapes until the margin
Exploded into an ear of sky. Today the hospitals
Are light, airy places, tented clouds, and the weeping
In corridors is like autumn showers. It's beginning.

*

Unless this is the shelf of whatever happens? The cold sun-
rise attacks one side of the giant capital letters, bestirs a
little the landmass as it sinks, grateful but asleep. And you
too are a rebus from another century, your fiction in piles
like lace, in that a new way of appreciating has been in-
vented, that tomorrow will be quantitatively and qualita-
tively different—young love, cheerful, insubstantial things
—and that these notions have been paraded before, though
never with the flashing density climbing higher with you on
the beanstalk until the jewelled mosaic of hills, ploughed
fields and rivers agreed to be so studied and fell away for-
ever, a gash of laughter, a sneeze of gold dust into the prism
that weeps and remains solid.

Well had she represented the patient's history to his apa-
thetic scrutiny. Always there was something to see, some-
thing going on, *for the historical past owed it to itself, our
historical present.* There were visiting firemen, rumors of
chattels on a spree, old men made up to look like young
women in the polygon of night from which light sometimes
breaks, to be sucked back, armies of foreigners who could
not understand each other, the sickening hush just before the
bleachers collapse, the inevitable uninvited and only guest
who writes on the wall: I choose not to believe. It became a
part of oral history. Things overheard in cafés assumed an
importance previously reserved for letters from the front.

The past was a dream of doctors and drugs. This wasn't misspent time. Oh, sometimes it'd seem like doing the same thing over and over, until I had passed beyond whatever the sense of it had been. Besides, hadn't it all ended a long time back, on some clear, washed-out afternoon, with a stiff breeze that seemed to shout: go back! For the moated past lives by these dreams of decorum that take into account any wisecracks made at their expense. It is not called living in a past. If history were only minding one's business, but, once under the gray shade of mist drawn across us . . . And who am I to speak this way, into a shoe? I know that evening is busy with lights, cars . . . That the curve will include me if I must stand here. My warm regards are cold, falling back to the vase again like a fountain. Responsible to whom? I have chosen this environment and it is handsome: a festive ruching of bare twigs against the sky, masks under the balconies

that

I sing alway